Acknowledgments
This book was compiled by Lynne Bradbury from
the film adaptation by Dianne Jackson, *Supervising Director;*
Dave Unwin, *Director;* John Coates, *Producer;*
Iain Harvey, *Executive Producer;*
Gower Frost, Co-*Executive Producer.*
Lyrics by Ian Llande.

Ladybird books are widely available, but in case of
difficulty may be ordered by post or telephone from:

Ladybird Books – Cash Sales Department
Littlegate Road Paignton Devon TQ3 3BE
Telephone 01803 554761

A catalogue record for this book is available
from the British Library

Published by Ladybird Books Ltd Loughborough Leicestershire UK
Father Christmas is a TVC London production
© RAYMOND BRIGGS/BLOOMING PRODUCTIONS 1991/1994
LADYBIRD and the device of a Ladybird are trademarks of Ladybird Books Ltd

Raymond Briggs'
Father Christmas

Last Christmas morning Father Christmas had come home feeling very tired, freezing cold – and more grumpy than ever. He was so fed up that he decided it was time to take a holiday.

First he turned his sledge into a caravan for the reindeer to pull, and then he packed his suitcases.

When it was time to leave, Father Christmas took Cat and Dog to the kennels and sadly said goodbye. He hitched the reindeer to the front of the sledge and off they flew…

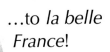

…to *la belle France*!

So that no one would recognise him, Father Christmas bought a stripey jumper and a beret.

"Right then, dinner time!" he thought. "Lovely, fish! What – no chips?"

After that came lobster, snails *and* pudding, followed by the bill. "Crumbs!" he cried. "Bloomin' expensive!"

La Glorieux

Father Christmas had eaten so much that he began to feel very poorly!

A few days later some people at the campsite discovered the reindeer. "Hmmm! Time to move on," mumbled Father Christmas. "I know – I'll go to *Scotland*!"

He landed in a valley in the pouring rain.
"B-b-bloomin' c-c-cold," shivered Father
Christmas and he went to an inn to warm
up. He loved the bagpipes and dancing.

Next morning the sun was shining, and
he jumped into the loch for a swim.
"Aaaargh! It's freezin'. Enough's enough!
I need to go somewhere *hot*!"

Las Vegas! Nice room. Good food. Plenty to do. *"This is the life!"* chuckled Father Christmas.

And so the days and weeks went by.

One morning, by the pool, a small boy recognised who he was.

"Oh, dear!" moaned Father Christmas. "Time to be off again."

He asked for his bill. It was *enormous*! "Better go home," he said. So he packed his bags and set off.

"Back again, m'deers!" And the caravan bumped on the ground. "Better go and get the rascals."

Cat and Dog were so excited to see him again. "All right! All right! Mind me bloomin' beard!" laughed Father Christmas.

As he tried to push his front door open, Father Christmas found a mountain of letters behind it. "Bloomin' Christmas post already!" he grumbled. "Gets earlier every year." But he still sat down to read every single one.

His list of presents grew longer, and each morning more letters arrived.

Soon it was time to get his suit from the dry cleaners. The lady in the shop who served him thought he was going to a fancy dress party.

"I should be so lucky," he growled at her.

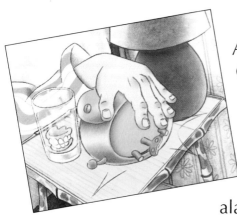

At last it was Christmas Eve, and Father Christmas was woken early by his noisy alarm clock.

"Bloomin' Christmas here again," he moaned, crawling out of bed, and pulling back the curtains to look out. "Uggh! It's snowed during the night." And he carried on grumbling as he got dressed.

He fed
Cat and Dog
and listened to the
weather forecast. "S'pose
I'd better load up the sledge," he said.
Then he fetched the reindeer and
harnessed them up.

Snow began to
fall again as
he gently
steered
the sledge
through his
open gate.

"Tally-ho, m'deers!" he cheered, and the sledge took off into the sky.

But Father Christmas soon started complaining again when he flew straight through a thunderstorm. So to cheer himself up a little, he began to sing a song:

Jump up on my sleigh,
And we're all on our way,
To another bloomin' Christmas!

His sledge landed on the roof of the first house, and Father Christmas squeezed down the chimney. He crept softly into the children's bedroom and carefully tucked the presents into their stockings.

Throughout the night Father Christmas and the reindeer flew from place to place.

His biggest problem was how to get into some of the houses. Some chimneys were a really tight squeeze. "Oooh!" moaned Father Christmas. Other places didn't have any chimneys at all!

Father Christmas took a break and listened to the weather forecast again. Then it was back to work.

"That's it, boys," he said to the reindeer some time after. "We'd better get a move on. We're a bit late for the party this year."

There was cheering and waving as the sledge landed in the middle of the Snowman Party.

"Hello, James!" said Father Christmas to a little boy with a snowman. "Glad you could make it again this year."

The party was wonderful, with plenty of food and dancing. Then James and his snowman went to see the reindeer and to find *their* presents in the sledge. But, oh dear! They found two more hidden under the seat.

"That's torn it!" said Father Christmas. "I've left the wrong present before, but I've never *forgotten* any. Come on, m'deers, we're going for the bloomin' record! Bye, all. See you next year!"

"Come on! We're nearly there now," he shouted, as they flew over London and into the grounds of Buckingham Palace. "Oh, good! Flag's flying – they're in!" He quietly delivered the last two parcels and headed back to the sledge.

"Still at it, mate?" asked the milkman.

"Done now, thank bloomin' goodness," growled Father Christmas.

And he and the reindeer set off for home.

"Well done, m'deers,"
he said, as they
landed safely.
He yawned and
led the reindeer
to their stable.

Once inside his warm
house, Father Christmas
took off his hat and
boots.

He hung up hi jacket and then made himself a nice cup of tea.

He rolled up his sleeves and, with Cat sitting on his shoulders, he prepared the Christmas dinner.

When everything was cooked he sat down to enjoy it.

Later, after
Father Christmas
had had a steaming
hot bath,
he got ready for bed.

He put a parcel each
for Dog and Cat
under the tree and
picked up his own
presents. Then
Father Christmas
headed upstairs.

"Might as well open them now," he thought, looking at the first present. "Mind you, I already know what's in this one – another bloomin' awful tie from Auntie Edie.

"The usual *ghastly* socks from Cousin Violet," he grumbled, unwrapping the second.

"Phew! That's more like it," Father Christmas laughed, as he discovered a bottle. "Good old Uncle Bob!"

Father Christmas leaned over to change the date on the calendar. It was Christmas Day. "Well, that's that for another bloomin' year," he said thankfully.

"And a happy bloomin' Christmas to you and all!"

Poor old Father Christmas,
He never sees Christmas morn,
He works so hard on Christmas Eve,
He's asleep before the dawn.

Dear old Father Christmas,
We think you're very kind,
And if you get a little grumpy,
We don't really mind!

Thank you, Father Christmas,
From every boy and girl,
And all the children everywhere
In the whole wide bloomin' world.